First published in the United States, Great Britain, Canada, Australia, and New Zealand in 2011 by North-South Books Inc.,
an imprint of NordSüd Verlag AG, CH-8005 Zürich, Switzerland.
Distributed in the United States by North-South Books Inc., New York 10001.

Library of Congress Cataloging-in-Publication Data is available.
ISBN: 978-0-7358-4043-0 (trade edition)
Printed in China by Leo Paper Products Ltd., Heshan, Guangdong, May 2011.
1 3 5 7 9 · 10 8 6 4 2

www.northsouth.com

Lieve Baeten

Happy Birthday,
Little Witch!

NorthSouth
New York / London

It was Lizzy the Little Witch's birthday. And what would a birthday be without a cake?

Lizzy tried to conjure up one, but the spell didn't work. Lizzy guessed she would have to buy a cake instead. So off she flew to the Witch Village Market.

"Cat! Cat! Where are you?" Lizzy called when she got home. "Come see the gorgeous cake I've bought." But Cat was nowhere to be seen.

"Maybe she's in Witch Village," Lizzy thought. So back she flew to have a look.

First she flew to the Witch Village Market, where there were lots of good things that not only witches like but cats like too.

"Hello! It's me, back again!" Lizzy called to the witches inside. "Have you seen my cat?
She needs to come home because it's my birthday, and we're having a party tonight."

"You poor thing!" said the witch in green. "Have you lost your cat? She's not here. And I'm afraid we have no time at all to help you look for her."

"That's all right," said Lizzy. "Maybe I'll find Cat in the Witch This-'n'-That Shop."

And wasn't that Lizzy's cat up there on the shelf, fast asleep?

No, it was just a pair of slippers.

"Hello!" said Lizzy to the witches inside. "I'm looking for my cat. It's my birthday, and we're having a party tonight."

"Your cat isn't here," said the witch in the blue apron. "And I'm afraid we have no time at all to help you look for her."

"That's all right," said Lizzy. "Cat is probably in the Witch Pet Store.

She loves to play with the rabbit and the turtle."

"Hello!" Lizzy called to the Pet Store Witch. "My cat has gone missing. Is she here with you?"

"No, I haven't seen your cat," said the Pet Store Witch. "And I'm afraid I have no time at all to help you look for her."

Where on earth could Cat have gone? Lizzy wondered. She had looked everywhere she could think of.

Lizzy felt awful. How could she enjoy her birthday cake without Cat?

Finally Lizzy flew home again, all alone, without her cat.

"Maybe Cat is hiding somewhere inside the house, waiting for me to come back,"
she thought hopefully.

It was so quiet inside, you could have heard a pin drop.

Everything looked exactly as it had before . . . or did it?

"For she's a jolly good fellow!
For she's a jolly good fellow!"
What a surprise! All the witches were there. And they'd brought lots of presents with them:
a witch's cloak, a magic wand, a new book of spells, and a crystal ball.

"Now watch carefully," said Lizzy as she waved her magic wand.

"Abracadabra, Abracadat.

Come home to me now,

my dear little cat!"

And *POOF!* The best birthday present of all.